The Princess and the Badger

Just Right Reader

Amber loves playing with blocks. So does her brother, Roger.

Before dinner, Amber made a castle. Roger prefers to make badgers.

After dinner, Amber catches a person yelling. It's coming from the corner of the den where she and Roger were. She enters and sees Roger's badger chasing someone from her castle!

Amber is very mixed up. The person and badger are made of blocks! Hmm, can this be?

The person hollers, "Help me! The badger is after me! I can't run much longer!"

"Roger! Come and look!" Amber says.

Roger enters just as the badger is on the verge of catching the princess.

Amber grabs some blocks and makes a ladder. The princess runs up it and perches on the top. The badger can't get to her!

Roger says to his sister, "Very clever!"

But the badger never gives up! It jumps over the side of the castle.

The princess is perching on one of the corners.

"It's going to get her!" yells Amber.

Roger grabs and jerks the badger.
There is only one way to stop it!

Roger takes the blocks apart. The
badger will never enter the castle now!

Amber thanks her brother.

Amber whispers, "You are no longer suffering."

Roger snickers.

"It's better if I make my badgers somewhere else. It's safer."

Amber nods.

"But just in case, I will put my castle on the rim of a lake."

"Very clever," says Roger.

Phonics Fun

Write 2 sentences using words from the word list in the book.

Comprehension

Why do you think Roger says it would be better if he built his badgers somewhere safer?

High Frequency Words

there very where

Decodable Words

after	never
badger	over
better	perch
brother	person
clever	prefer
corner	safer
dinner	sister
enter	snicker
her	suffer
holler	verge
jerk	were
ladder	whisper
longer	